ICE HOCKEY LEGENDS

Martin Brodeur

Sergei Fedorov

Peter Forsberg

Wayne Gretzky

Dominik Hasek

Brett Hull

Jaromir Jagr

Paul Kariya

John LeClair

Mario Lemieux

Eric Lindros

Mark Messier

CHELSEA HOUSE PUBLISHERS

ICE HOCKEY LEGENDS

JOHN LECLAIR

Phelan Powell

CHELSEA HOUSE PUBLISHERS
Philadelphia

Produced by P. M. Gordon Associates
Philadelphia, Pennsylvania

Picture research by Gillian Speeth, Picture This

CHELSEA HOUSE PUBLISHERS

Editor in Chief: Stephen Reginald
Managing Editor: James Gallagher
Production Manager: Pamela Loos
Art Director: Sara Davis
Director of Photography: Judy L. Hasday
Senior Production Editor: Lisa Chippendale
Publishing Coordinator: James McAvoy
Project Editor: Becky Durost Fish
Cover Design and Digital Illustration: Keith Trego

Cover Photos: AP/Wide World Photos

The Chelsea House World Wide Web site address is
http://www.chelseahouse.com

First Printing

1 3 5 7 9 8 6 4 2

Library of Congress Cataloging-in-Publication Data

Powell, Phelan.
John LeClair / Phelan Powell.
p. cm. — (Ice hockey legends)
Includes bibliographical references (p.) and index.
Summary: A biography of John LeClair, the player who helped the Philadelphia Flyers reach the Stanley Cup finals in 1997 and who played in the 1998 Olympics in Nagano, Japan.
ISBN 0-7910-5016-5 (hc)
1. LeClair, John, 1969- —Juvenile literature. 2. Hockey players—United States—Biography—Juvenile literature. 3. Philadelphia Flyers (Hockey team)—Juvenile literature. [1. LeClair, John, 1969- . 2. Hockey players.] I. Title. II. Series.
GV848.5.L43P57 1998
796.962'092—dc21 98-45023
[B] CIP
AC

CONTENTS

SHER-WOOD
SHERWOOD

1 His Personal Best

John LeClair skated into the power play intent on scoring.

That drive to score had been with him ever since he was a boy in Vermont, playing on junior hockey teams. The roar of the crowd when he got the puck into the net was something that he loved. The fans from the tiny town of St. Albans, Vermont, wanted little Johnny LeClair to score, and they rewarded him grandly with their cheers when he did.

Now, on April 13, 1998, he was in his third full season with the Philadelphia Flyers, and he had his eye on the goal that would give him his third consecutive season of 50 or more goals. But the Dominator—the Buffalo Sabres' formidable Dominik Hasek—was guarding the goal like a dragon at the entrance of a castle. How sweet it would

In March 1998, en route to his third straight season of 50 or more goals, John LeClair battles for the puck with Scott Stevens of the New Jersey Devils.

be for LeClair to score his 50th against such a talented and fierce opponent!

At the 1998 winter Olympics in Nagano, Japan, Hasek had played for the Czech Republic, the team that won the gold medal, and the Czech fans had chanted, "Hasek je Buh" (Hasek is God). But LeClair had no fear of this god who was standing between him and his goal.

Buffalo Sabre Alexei Zhitnik tried to capture the puck but overskated as John LeClair zoomed up to it. LeClair pushed it to and fro across the ice, moving ever closer to the net. In an instant LeClair saw a crack in Hasek's defenses, and he fired. The flashing puck evaded Hasek's gloved hand. The goal was LeClair's!

With that goal John LeClair became the first American-born player in NHL history to score 50 or more goals in three consecutive seasons. Known for his strong and deadly shots, he had once again established his reputation as one of the National Hockey League's top scorers.

In that game on April 13, the Flyers shot 31 times against Hasek, and LeClair was the only Flyer to score. Hasek's dominance in the net would come back to haunt the Flyers during their postseason playoff games against the Sabres.

For the moment, though, LeClair could enjoy his personal triumph. When asked how he felt about scoring his 50th goal, he was characteristically humble. "It's a different accomplishment to be the first American," he said in a postgame interview. But he added, "A lot of it has to do with team play and having opportunities."

It had taken some time for those opportunities to arrive. In 1987, during his senior year of high school, LeClair was drafted by the Montreal Canadiens. But instead of signing a professional contract and playing in the minors, he decided to attend the University of Vermont. After his college career, when he finally did join the Canadiens, he became the first native of Vermont to play for an NHL team.

In his very first game with the Canadiens, on March 9, 1991, LeClair scored a goal. In 1993 the Canadiens won the Stanley Cup, the league's championship trophy, thanks to two consecutive overtime goals by LeClair. Nevertheless, his years with the Canadiens were plagued with injuries that forced him to miss numerous games, and his career seemed to stall at times.

Since being traded to the Flyers in 1995, LeClair

April 13, 1998: About to score his 50th goal of the season, LeClair takes the puck down the ice.

has stayed healthy, and his talents have blossomed. Besides his scoring achievements, he was selected for the NHL All-Star Game in each of his first three full years with the Flyers.

His success in Philadelphia came as a surprise to some. LeClair had played as a center with Montreal, but when he came to Philadelphia he was assigned to play left wing on a line with Eric Lindros and Mikael Renberg. Flyers general manager Bob Clarke had no idea how well this trio would perform on the ice. "We figured we would try [LeClair] first with Eric," Clarke remembered, "and if that didn't work, we'd move Rod Brind'Amour to the first and use John at center on the second line." In fact, with their combined size, strength, and skill, Lindros, Renberg, and LeClair soon became a dominant line, nicknamed the "Legion of Doom."

His success on that line, and his great burst of goal scoring, did not lead LeClair to slack off. Every sport has its ghosts, and LeClair was afraid he might be a reincarnation of Warren Young. Young was a winger for the Pittsburgh Penguins who had a 40-goal season one year when he played on a line with NHL great Mario Lemieux. When he was taken off that line, his output dropped to about 10 goals a season.

"The thing that drives me most is not embarrassing myself," LeClair revealed. "Not being a joke like Warren Young, not having people use my name like that. That drives me more than self-doubt. No one likes to be embarrassed. I scored some goals [51] my first full year here [with Philadelphia]. It was important for me to back it up the next season. It's the next year that says a lot about you."

At 6'3" and 226 pounds, LeClair is always a threat around the net.

Now he is well beyond being labeled a one-year wonder, but LeClair continues to demand the most of himself. He is one of the league's biggest and most powerful players, standing 6'3" and weighing in at 226 pounds. A mighty warrior on the blades, he will continue to be a big force in the NHL for years to come.

LeCLAIR
9
KOHO

HOME, SWEET HOME

John LeClair was born on July 5, 1969, in the town of St. Albans, Vermont, close to the Canadian border. The town, near beautiful Lake Champlain, has not changed much since the 1950s. It is a homey place with a town square in the middle of Main Street.

John's father, Butch LeClair, managed a paint store in St. Albans for many years. Butch's own parents had lived in a number of places in New England and upstate New York before settling in St. Albans in 1942.

John's mother, Beverly, is a surgical nurse at the Northwest Medical Center in St. Albans. John has three older sisters: Mary Kay, a homemaker who lives in Cleveland; Nancy, a high school teacher in Marlton, New Jersey; and Susan, a chef in Seattle. John's younger brother, Joe, is in the Peace Corps, working in the Ivory Coast in western Africa.

By his freshman year at the University of Vermont, LeClair's skating had greatly improved. His new skills, combined with his size and strength, made him a potent offensive player.

How did this family, and this small town, produce such a hockey player? Though John's father was familiar with the game, he had never played hockey himself. In fact, there were no organized hockey teams in the St. Albans area until the 1960s. When John was born, the sport was just becoming recognized in the region.

Hockey was visible enough, though, for John to notice it. When he was six years old, he asked his father for some hockey skates.

Butch remembered where the kids went to play their hearts out in those early days: "At first, they played in an old railroad shed. Then they got a bunch of people who signed a note and built Coote Field Arena. It was just a metal shack with a lunch bar and an old tractor to scrape the ice. It was kind of primitive, but it worked very well. It produced some good hockey."

That was how John started. "He liked to score right away," Butch recalled, "because when he scored, everybody cheered. He thought that was a good thing."

Skating was not one of young John's strong points. "He just wasn't a very good skater," said Butch. "He was always on his ankles and he had an awful time. That was a big problem at first."

Luke Cioffi also remembers John LeClair's early years in hockey. Cioffi and LeClair were six years old when they started playing together, and they played on the same line at their high school, Bellows Free Academy. "Skating wasn't one of his highlights," Cioffi recalled, laughing. "That blue line was just too thick for him some days."

It took John several years to develop into a better skater. In the meantime, he scored goals in any way he could—on his knees, if necessary. John's eyes were always on the net.

Heather Streeter, who now works for the St. Albans Chamber of Commerce, is another who remembers the young LeClair. "I played on a team with John when we were little," she recounted. "I was the goalie, and I had a 0.82 goals-against average—because with John on my team, the puck was always at the other end."

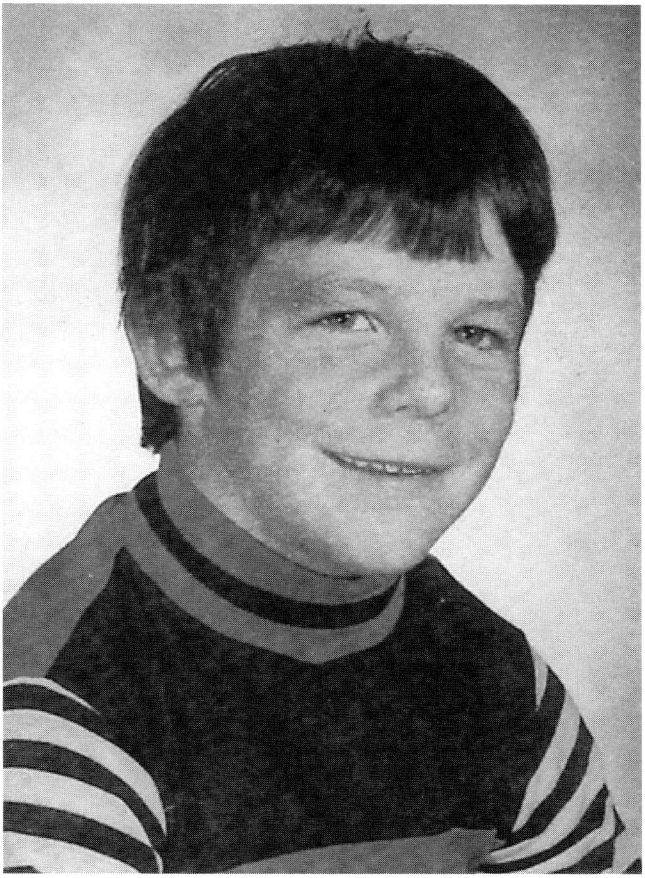

The fourth of five children, John LeClair grew up in the town of St. Albans, Vermont.

Hockey became a round-the-clock pursuit for John. He and his friends would play during the day on weekends and then play some more at night. One of his frequent companions on the rink was Jeremy Benoit, whose father, Richard, created a homemade rink for the youngsters. Flooding his yard with water from a nearby creek, the elder Benoit added boards around the edge and installed lights for night play. He remembers how wrapped up in the game the kids became: "Sometimes they'd still be out there at midnight on a school night. We'd have to chase them."

For Butch LeClair the scene in the Benoit yard remains vivid: "It was a volleyball court in the summer. But in the winter, he'd flood it. There were boards and lights, and the kids would play all night. They even had a little shack with a heater there so that when they got too cold, they could go inside and warm up."

When John LeClair was a freshman at Bellows Free Academy, he still did not skate well enough to make the school's hockey team. But he continued to play in community leagues, and despite his weak skating skills, he continued to score.

In his sophomore year John was ready for the Bellows team, and its members were ready for him. "We'd be dumping the puck in [during a change of lines]," remembered Luke Cioffi, "and there would be John, in the corner on his knees and hands, five against one, somehow getting the puck out of the corner."

Continual improvement has been a hallmark of John's career, and it was evident in high school. College scouts started looking at the young LeClair. As a junior, he played at the Hockey Night in Boston, a showcase for young talent. The scouts were impressed with this big winger from Vermont.

But it was not just the college scouts who were watching John LeClair. When John was a senior in 1987, the Montreal Canadiens drafted him to play in the minors. John decided to go to college first, and he was accepted at the University of Vermont (UVM).

Mark Toof, affectionately known as "Toofie," was a college teammate. Now a high school teacher and hockey coach in St. Albans, Toof grew up with LeClair and shared many hours with him on the ice. According to Toof, John never talked at that time about wanting to play in the NHL. "It was a big deal for someone from St. Albans [just] to go to UVM. He's only the second player from here to go to UVM."

John's father, Butch, thinks John never talked about playing in the NHL because of a concern that, if he failed, people would give him a hard time. If that was the case, John need not have worried.

"He was just one of those guys that blossomed late," said Toby Ducolon, who played with LeClair in college and now coaches at Bellows Free Academy. "He was a good high school player, an excellent college player, and a great pro player. By the time he got to college, he was a good puck handler, could see the ice, and was very strong on his skates. Over time, he developed into the full package. I think that's one of his biggest assets. He continues to improve. That's half the reason he's worth what he's worth. Some people peak early. He's still improving."

In a recent interview Luke Cioffi talked about how St. Albans, a small town of 12,000 hard-working citizens, has supported John LeClair's aspirations. "Around here, it's always been, 'Hey, John, go for it. If that's what you want, we'll do what we can for you.' The whole community, the whole state, has taken that same attitude. His parents always said, 'Hey, we're going to do what we can for you. It may not be the best, but we expect you to try your hardest.' The kids around here are taught that. Especially with hockey. 'Do your best and whatever you get out of it is great.'"

Jamey Horan also attended Bellows Free Academy with LeClair. He remembers John's intense focus as a hockey player. "He's not happy until the puck is in the net, and it doesn't have to be him," said Horan. "He's just as happy to dish the puck off. It's like a period at the end of a sentence for him."

LeClair did the best he could at UVM, even though his sports career there was hampered by injuries. The professional scouts were not bothered by the fact that he played only 28 games dur-

In his senior year at Vermont, LeClair was the team's leading scorer and an Eastern Collegiate Athletic Association second-team All-Star.

ing his sophomore and junior years. In his senior year at UVM, he showed the promise the Canadiens knew he had. After being sidelined for the first month of the season with meningitis, LeClair scored 25 goals and racked up 20 assists in a mere 33 games. This is what the pros were waiting for.

Butch LeClair recalled the frequent visits the NHL scouts would make to the family's home in

St. Albans. "It was the same thing every summer," he said. "They would say to John, 'You've had enough of this college hockey. Why don't you come play with us?' John would say, 'No.' He wanted to finish college."

A Stick and a Promise

It was not until John LeClair left the University of Vermont that the National Hockey League finally got hold of him. He went to play for the Montreal Canadiens in 1991.

His professional debut did not win instant glory for the young man. In fact, he had a hard time on the ice, particularly with his skating. It was as if he had grown into his huge body before he learned how to use it to his advantage.

LeClair's hometown fans and relatives would often make the short trip from St. Albans to Montreal to see him play. His performance usually ended up being nothing anybody would want to talk about. When LeClair came home, he would not complain about his games, but everyone knew he was not having a good time.

Kevin Smith, who owns a sporting goods store on Main Street in St. Albans, hasn't forgotten that

LeClair hoists the NHL's championship trophy, the Stanley Cup. Although he was not an instant star in the league, by his third year he helped the Montreal Canadiens win the Cup.

time: "In Montreal, when they were calling him inconsistent and saying he didn't come to play every night, it really wore on him and bothered him."

John's father also remembers: "He was close enough to home that that provided him with a little security in those years. But it's still a growing-up period for a kid, and that's hard to do in the National Hockey League. Even for a 21-year-old. I feel sorry for all those kids in the league who are only 18. It must be awful for them."

At one point, during a practice for the 1993 Stanley Cup playoffs, LeClair bumbled into a teammate, who ended up sliding into the Canadiens' coach, Jacques Demers. This might have been seen as a symbol of all LeClair's struggles as a professional. Luckily, though, Demers did not mind a great deal. In fact, by this time, he was the only one on the team who believed LeClair had yet to reach his full potential. While everyone else was wondering why this kid was on a professional hockey team, Demers had the perception, born of experience, to predict that LeClair would be the next Kevin Stevens. At that time Stevens had scored 50 goals in two consecutive seasons.

Demers's faith was borne out in those 1993 playoffs, when LeClair scored two consecutive overtime goals for the Canadiens against the Los Angeles Kings to clinch the Stanley Cup. "John LeClair," said Demers, "is going to be a star in this league. I told him a few months ago he's going to be a very wealthy man."

The Stanley Cup, originally donated by Lord Stanley, a governor-general of Canada, is the oldest trophy in any of today's professional sports. It is also the only one that the winning team can take home until the next year's competition. Any

LeClair (standing to the left of the trophy, leaning toward it) joins his Canadiens teammates in celebrating their 1993 Stanley Cup win.

player on the team can borrow the Cup to show his hometown. This practice has led to some strange occurrences. One year the Stanley Cup ended up at the bottom of player Mario Lemieux's swimming pool. Back in 1924, when some members of the Montreal Canadiens were carrying the Cup in a Model T Ford, they had to get out to push the car up a hill, and when they clambered back in and drove away, they left the Cup on the side of the road.

John LeClair was more careful with the Cup. When it was his turn to have the trophy, he was excited and proud to take it home to St. Albans. In that town of 12,000 citizens, 10,000 people filled the Collins Perley sports center to see their hero and the Stanley Cup, get his autograph, and have their picture taken with him.

Patrick Leahy, a Democratic senator from Vermont, remembers meeting LeClair on the day that was proclaimed John LeClair Day. "He said to me, 'I'm John LeClair.' I said, 'I know who you are.' He said I had to hold the Stanley Cup [because] 'it's neat.' Whatever he gets, there's no jealousy; there's just pride."

For the celebration, Leahy hand-delivered a letter to John from President Bill Clinton. In the letter, the president congratulated LeClair for his win and praised him for his dedication to the sport

Converted to left wing after his trade to the Philadelphia Flyers, LeClair immediately showed his new team his rough-and-tumble style.

of hockey. Clinton also said he was proud that John was the first citizen of Vermont to play in the National Hockey League.

It was not just John LeClair's starring role in the Stanley Cup win that brought so many residents of St. Albans to the sports arena. They were especially willing to honor LeClair because he had stayed connected to his hometown and its people. He had returned home often, keeping in touch with old friends. He had frequently taken friends and relatives to the Canadiens' locker room.

Vermont governor Howard Dean remembers the time LeClair invited him and his two children to a game. The Deans were already big LeClair fans, and they were even more impressed by the way John treated them. "He's very unpretentious, very easy to be with," said Dean. "I wish there were a lot more stories about people like him in sports. He brings real credit to professional sports."

"Vermont is like a small town," Dean continued. "The whole state feels the same way about him that St. Albans does."

Senator Leahy echoed these sentiments: "John's a true Vermonter. He's never forgotten where he's from. He's a Cal Ripken kind of person. I've been around athletes who are extremely spoiled, but John isn't that way. As a result, people can share in his joy."

That year was the high point of LeClair's career with Montreal. Less than two years later, on February 9, 1995, he was traded to the Philadelphia Flyers, where he would wear the number 10 on his orange, black, and white jersey.

Converted from center to left wing, LeClair was put on a line with Eric Lindros and Mikael Renberg. The three immediately clicked as a force that would be hard to beat. In a February 14 game

Eric Lindros celebrates with LeClair after scoring a goal. Together on the same line, Lindros and LeClair formed one of the league's most powerful duos.

against the Tampa Bay Lightning, the Flyers won, 5–2, and LeClair scored three goals—a hat trick.

His first goal as a Flyer came in the initial period. John then assisted Renberg on two goals. Said Renberg after the game, "I've got to give a lot of credit to John and Eric. John is a hell of a player. If we work hard together, we're going to have a good game."

By the third period, the Lightning had bounced back from a lackluster performance to bring the score to 3–2. But LeClair got physical, muscling in close to the net. Just 56 seconds into the period, he knocked a defenseman down before skirting by another, and he slammed the puck past Lightning goalie Daren Puppa.

LeClair's third goal, giving him the hat trick, was the easiest. He shot the puck into an empty net.

Lindros, the reigning star of the team, voiced appreciation for his fellow linemen after the game: "I'm behind them all the time, just hanging on their coattails. John is so strong driving through, there aren't a whole lot of people who can stop him."

EASTERN
SHER-W
SHER-
THE

4 Cool Running

As a hockey player, John LeClair really came alive in Philadelphia, as if it were now time to fulfill Jacques Demers's prophecy. Just 12 days after his first hat trick with the Flyers, LeClair did it again. This time it was against his old teammates, the Montreal Canadiens.

LeClair went into the game just hoping to play well in front of his former fans. But he excelled on the ice, and the fans went wild when he scored his third goal in the final period. They tossed their hats onto the ice by the hundreds. The Flyers shut out the Canadiens, 7–0.

Flyers coach Terry Murray kept his hat but was elated with the new guy on his team. "He's fired up right now," said Murray after the game. "Trades do that to people. We're very happy that he's excited."

Linemate Eric Lindros praised LeClair's skills on the ice. "He goes right to the net, and the puck

LeClair warms up for his first All-Star Game in January 1996.

Playing for Team USA, LeClair tangles with Canadian goaltender Curtis Joseph during Game 3 of the 1996 World Cup finals. The United States won the game and the series.

is generally there for him," said Lindros. "He's incredible how he's going."

Within three weeks of being traded from Montreal to Philadelphia, LeClair had been named the NHL player of the week. He had 14 points in seven games with his new team.

In a short time the Lindros-LeClair-Renberg line was dubbed the Legion of Doom, and the trio lived up to their name. Coach Murray was particularly happy because LeClair and Renberg, both sturdy players, prevented opponents from concentrating on Lindros, who became a prime target when he was teamed with smaller linemen.

LeClair knew the opportunity was ripe for him to excel. "One thing you won't hear me say is that I never got a chance," he declared. "This is my chance. I've got to take advantage of it."

He admitted he had been invigorated by the trade. "Things are a lot different here," he told reporters. "It's great to be back playing hockey. It felt like hockey wasn't as fun for me [in Montreal]. I'm really enjoying it."

Aside from his emotional high, he felt there were reasons on the ice for his greater success in Philadelphia than in Montreal. "Here, they're a little more open to the offensive game," he explained. "In Montreal, it's defense first. This style has really helped me a lot. I've had more chances since I've been here than I had all season [with Montreal]. Every game here I've had a very good opportunity to score."

His old supporter, Canadiens coach Jacques Demers, was ecstatic for his protégé. "I'm just happy for him," Demers said after his team had been trounced by the Flyers, 8–4, "because he's an honest kid, a down-to-earth kid, he doesn't have a big ego. . . . I saw [his potential for stardom], but we couldn't get it out of him because we had him at center and he should have been at left wing."

At this point, John LeClair saw only one bad thing about his trade. "I'm getting too much publicity," he told reporters.

And LeClair continued to draw publicity. The next season, 1995–96, he began his string of years with 50 or more goals and selection to the All-Star Game. In 1996 he also went to the World Cup games, where his U.S. team brought the Canadian team to its knees. LeClair's dominance on the ice made him a standout during the competition.

By 1997, when he played in his second All-Star Game, LeClair was considered by many to be the NHL's top wingman. That year, when Lindros missed a number of games because of injury, LeClair became the Flyers' chief scorer. Teammate Mikael Renberg spoke of LeClair's vital contributions to the team. "He's a great two-way player," Renberg said. "He's strong in our zone, and along the boards. . . . He's really hard on himself. If our line is playing bad, he always takes it on his shoulders. He's a great role model for the younger guys, like Dainius Zubrus and Janne Niinimaa, to show them what it takes to be a great athlete."

Ron Hextall, a Flyers goalie, was equally impressed with LeClair's efforts: "If you sat there for one game and just watched Johnny, you'd be amazed by the cross-checks, the slashes and the spears he takes when he's in front of the net. He really pays the price. But he's absolutely possessed to score goals. If he wasn't as possessed as he is, he'd be a 20-goal scorer instead of a 50-goal scorer. Besides, he's big and strong with arms like oak trees. You just can't defend him."

In 1997 the Philadelphia Flyers surged all the

way to the finals of the Stanley Cup playoffs, but they fell just short of winning the championship. LeClair was disappointed, especially because he remembered his elation after Montreal's victory in 1993: "I'll never forget the feeling of winning the Cup; it's a tremendous achievement, one of the greatest experiences I've had in hockey. That's what makes me want to win the Cup even more now; because I know what it's like, it's a real incentive."

LeClair went into the next season, 1997–98, hoping the Flyers would have another chance at the elusive Stanley Cup. But that year would bring a different kind of thrill—the chance to play for his country during the 1998 winter Olympics in Nagano, Japan.

10
CANADA
KOHO

IN THE EYES OF THE WORLD

John LeClair's expertise helped the U.S. team beat the Canadian team to win the World Cup finals in 1996. In Game 2 of the three-game series, LeClair scored off a slapshot during the first period, tying the score. Then, in the second period, John did it again—directing another slapshot into the net to put his team ahead.

Buoyed by this victory, the United States went on to win the third game and the series. In the three games, LeClair had a total of six goals and four assists. The Canadian team members and their fans felt they had been bested at their own game, the game they had invented.

Two years later, at the 1998 Olympics, Team Canada still felt a need to right that terrible wrong. Again the Canadians would play Team USA, and they were looking for revenge.

In February 1998 the two rival teams took the long flight to Japan under different instructions

In the 1998 winter Olympics, LeClair was frequently found—as usual—in the face of the opponents' goaltender.

LeClair celebrates a goal in the 1996 World Cup finals. The U.S. victory there inspired the Canadian team to seek revenge at the 1998 Olympics.

from their respective coaches. The Canadian coach told his players not to sleep on the plane. He wanted them to be very tired by the time they reached their destination, so they could sleep before the games began.

Team USA, in contrast, was told to get some rest on the long trip. Two beds and an exercise bike were put on board. John LeClair watched three movies, *Forrest Gump*, *Men in Black*, and *Liar, Liar*, but he didn't use the exercise bike. "Don't tell anyone," he said, laughing, in a *Philadelphia Inquirer* interview.

LeClair was happy that the players on his team—the same group who had won the World Cup—already knew each other. He thought that would give the team an extra boost of confidence on the ice.

LeClair himself had a special incentive. His wife, Christina, who was back at their seasonal home in South Jersey, was due to deliver their second child during the Olympics. Thus, as the team's plane landed in Japan and the players set off for the Olympic Village, LeClair's hopes were high on several fronts.

At the most recent summer Olympics, in Atlanta,

the U.S. basketball team—the "Dream Team" players from the National Basketball Association (NBA)—had shunned the Olympic Village, instead choosing to stay in fancy hotels with all the expensive services, far from the other athletes. But LeClair and his teammates made the opposite decision. Although most of the NHL stars, like the NBA players, were millionaires, they elected to live in the Olympic Village with the rest of the athletes.

Without complaint, they unpacked their belongings in their tiny rooms. LeClair shared a room with four other players and slept on a bed that was far too short for his 6'3" body. There was no room service for the players. Each room had only a tiny television, with one English-language station.

But the excitement of being a part of the games overruled any discomfort the players may have felt. "For me," said LeClair, "part of participating is being part of the Olympic experience."

As for LeClair's roommates, their only complaint was about John's loud snoring. One player considered buying some earplugs in order to get a decent night's sleep.

The noise that Team USA was aching to hear was the roar of the fans. The players imagined the cheers that would erupt as they beat each team on the ice—particularly Team Canada. At first, as they passed one another in their walks around the village, the U.S. and Canadian team members nodded to each other. But as the games got underway, they ceased even that slight courtesy. They wanted to get into the "we're going to beat the pants off you" mode.

Many of the hockey teams that came to the Olympics were made up primarily of NHL stars who were playing for their country of birth. This was the first time NHL players had been allowed to participate in the Olympics. In earlier years the competition had been confined to amateurs.

Although the U.S. team was not traditionally a hockey power like the Canadians or the Russians, the Americans did have an Olympic heritage to live up to. At the 1960 Olympics in Squaw Valley, California, and again in 1980 at Lake Placid, New York, the U.S. team had surprised the world by winning the gold medal. John LeClair and his teammates, with their World Cup victory behind them, hoped to add to the American hockey legacy by capturing a third Olympic gold medal for their country.

LeClair predicted that the Americans' game against rival Team Canada would be particularly energetic. "I think the game with Canada will be a very physical one, with a lot of hitting," he said. "Just look at the players on the two teams. A lot has been built up about this. What happened in the World Cup obviously intensifies things a great deal."

First, however, LeClair and his team had to get past Team Sweden. Before the game with Sweden, LeClair commented on his opponents: "Some big boys there," he said to teammate Joel Otto. "Some pretty talented ones, too."

But LeClair felt confident. A big reason for his confidence was the Team USA goalie, Mike Richter, who was known as a thinking player. "That's the thing that sets him apart," said LeClair, "his smarts."

"We have faith in Mike. Why shouldn't we?" he added. "Look what he did in the World Cup."

Many of the outdoor Olympic events suffered delays from snowstorms, but the hockey teams did not have to wait for the weather to clear. On

February 13 Sweden and the United States took to the ice on schedule, in the building called the Big Hat, and at the end of the third period there was a winner and a loser.

Unfortunately for LeClair and his teammates, the game did not turn out as they had hoped. Their confidence and talent were not enough against Team Sweden, and they lost, 4–2.

The next day, Team USA came back to beat Team Belarus by a score of 5–2. John LeClair was credited with an assist when he drop-passed the puck to teammate Brian Leetch in the second period. Belarus was playing in its first Olympic Games, and the team had only two NHL players on its roster. Although the Americans scored on each of their five power plays, the Belarus team had a lot of confidence and played well.

By now, some players were commenting about problems with the rink. The Olympic hockey rink was several feet larger than a standard NHL rink. Other people were mentioning the thin air in Nagano, a town located more than 13,000 feet above sea level. In such conditions any athlete not used to high altitudes can suffer a loss of stamina. But John LeClair offered no such excuses for his team's less-than-impressive performance.

"We're trying to be too fancy," LeClair said. "We're thinking too much about the ice surface and playing differently instead of playing the way we know how. We've got to start taking the puck to the net, being more physical."

The showdown with Team Canada was scheduled for two days later. While the Americans had split their first two games, the Canadians had beaten Sweden and trounced Belarus. And besides their embarrassment about the World Cup loss, the Canadians had extra fuel to stoke their com-

In the U.S. game against Belarus at the 1998 Olympics, LeClair attempts to deflect the puck past goaltender Andrei Mezin. The Belarus team, in its first Olympics, played surprisingly well.

petitive fires. They were upset that the U.S. team had defenseman Gary Suter on the ice. In an NHL game right before the Olympics, Suter had been penalized for a high cross-check on Paul Kariya, one of the greatest stars in professional hockey. The hit gave Kariya a concussion that kept him from playing for Canada during the Olympic Games. The Canadians thought it unjust that Suter was playing while Kariya could not. The local Japanese fans were also irate because Kariya is partly Japanese by heritage.

In this charged atmosphere, the two teams took to the ice. There were more Canadian flags than American waving in the stands. Even personal friendships had to be set aside for this match. LeClair, for example, had to play tough against his own usual linemate, fellow Flyer Eric Lindros.

In the first period the two teams looked like they were just checking each other out. They played carefully. Canada scored one goal, the United States none.

The action really started in the second period, as both teams picked up speed and became more physical. Canada increased its lead to 2–0.

Team USA failed to take advantage of several power plays. Normally a team's best opportunity to score comes during a power play, when the other team has one or more players cooling their skates in the penalty box. But the Americans let these chances slip by.

In the third and final period, with a little more than five minutes left in the game, LeClair's team finally got on the scoreboard. As Team Canada's goalie Patrick Roy dropped low to block a shot from Brett Hull, Hull managed to hoist the puck over him. But that was small consolation as the game ended with a score of Canada 4, the United States 1.

LeClair maintained a positive attitude. "We played well," he said. "We have nothing to hang our heads about. Of course, it's disappointing to lose to Canada, but we continue to improve. We had numerous chances and had some bad breaks and did not put the puck in the net."

Looking ahead to the quarterfinals, he added: "Everyone is starting over. We feel confident we can still win the tournament."

Because Team USA ended up third in the round-robin portion of the competition, with a 1–2 record, the Americans would face the Czech Republic in the quarterfinals. At this point, if they did not win, they would be eliminated. The Czech team could not boast a huge number of NHL stars, but it did have the Dominator—goalie Dominik Hasek.

That season in the NHL, Hasek was on his way to winning the Hart Trophy as the league's most valuable player for the second consecutive year. So thin that people sometimes compared him to a scarecrow, Hasek was incredibly quick and flexible, able to stop shots that most goalies would never hope to reach. So far in the Olympics, he was giving up, on average, less than one goal per game.

Full of expectations, LeClair and his teammates took to the ice against the Czechs. Unluckily for them, Hasek lived up to his nickname, and the Czechs—who would go on to win the gold medal—crushed the Americans by a 4–1 score. The dejected American players left the ice at game's end with only the memory of the 1996 World Cup win to comfort them.

Although LeClair is not one to criticize the performance of others, he was disappointed with the

Canadian goalie Patrick Roy makes a kick-save against LeClair in the 1998 Olympic showdown. Failing to capitalize on its power plays, the U.S. team lost, 4–1.

team's play. "I don't see how anybody can go home," he declared, "and say we gave it our best shot." Personally, though he was just shy of having another 50-goal season in the NHL, he came away from the three Olympic games without a goal, and he was quick to shoulder his share of the blame.

"I can't make any excuses," he told the media.

"I just did not do the job. For whatever reason, I've got to take responsibility for that. It's embarrassing."

Eric Lindros—LeClair's Flyers teammate and Olympics opponent—insisted that John's performance in Nagano should not damage his solid reputation. "Everybody knows Johnny can score goals," said Lindros in a newspaper interview. "He's a great player."

Meanwhile, LeClair was expressing some frustration at having to listen to second-guessers, people who talked about the should-haves, would-haves, and could-haves. "Everybody's got the answers after everything is done. The way we prepared ourselves, in a short period of time, I don't know any other way you could have done it," said LeClair.

"Overall," LeClair summed up his experience, "I think I'll look back and still be honored that I had a chance to participate in the Olympics." Thinking ahead to the 2002 games to be held in Salt Lake City, Utah, he added, "I would definitely go [to the Olympics] again."

There was one additional heartache for LeClair and his U.S. teammates. Before the team left Nagano, one or more members apparently caused some damage in their living quarters. News reports the world over headlined stories about broken chairs and about fire extinguishers that were set off and thrown off the balcony. These stories marred the Americans' reputation far more than their less-than-inspiring showing on the ice.

John LeClair was not happy with all the media coverage of the incident. "I don't think we were the disgrace everyone said we were," he commented. "I know our room wasn't wrecked."

LeClair said he didn't know any details about

what happened, but he questioned the report about chairs being broken. "The thing I find surprising," he said, "is that everybody here is talking about the broken chairs. If anybody had sat on those tiny chairs, they'd know they broke on their own. One broke out from under me when I was playing cards."

The NHL was eventually made to pay about $3,000 to cover the damaged materials.

John LeClair tried to put the disappointments out of his mind. And one very positive thing had happened during his stay in Japan. Although he didn't have a gold medal to take home to his daughter, MacKenzie, he did have a new, nine-pound baby boy named Calvin waiting for him.

CCM
SHER-WOOD
SHER-WOOD
P.M.P. 7000

6

THE WINNING ATTITUDE

After the excitements and disappointments of the 1998 winter Olympics, the kid from St. Albans, Vermont, returned to his regular team, the Philadelphia Flyers, with another goal ahead of him: to help the Flyers capture the Stanley Cup, the prized trophy that the team had almost won during the previous season. The Flyers had fought to the death that year, only to be bested by the New Jersey Devils.

With so many players away in Japan, the NHL season had simply halted during the Olympics. The Philadelphia fans, like those in other NHL cities, were eager to have their team back home. But many Flyers fans were worried. Just before the break, the Flyers had struggled to a record of 6 losses in their last 8 games. With little time to regain their energy, they would now have to face 17 games during the month of March—a cruel schedule dictated by the league's need to make

John LeClair takes a break at a practice session during the 1998 playoffs. Although fierce on the ice, he knows how to keep the game in perspective.

up for lost time. Overall, the Flyers' record stood at 29–17–9, a few points lower than in the previous season.

But John LeClair thought that the experience of being in the Olympics—and winning only a single game there—would help him during the rest of the NHL season. "I had a lot of high hopes going into the Olympics," said LeClair. "Hopefully, I can channel that energy." He wanted to make up for the frustration at Nagano by taking the Stanley Cup on another visit to St. Albans.

As a team leader, LeClair tried to motivate his teammates by stating the goals clearly. "It's time for us to focus on what we've got to do," he said. "We've got to start playing better. We weren't playing well before the break, and it's time we start winning some games."

LeClair reported that Flyers coach Wayne Cashman had talked to the players about the condition of the team. "One thing he stressed, which is important, is that we don't accept losing," said LeClair. "We played a little better the last couple games before the break, but we didn't win, and that's not good enough."

As for the heavy load of 17 games in one month, LeClair characteristically took it in stride: "It can be the easiest month, if we play well. We can make it one of the best months or one of the worst."

Spring came earlier than usual to Philadelphia in 1998. People said it was the famous weather phenomenon El Niño that was causing flowers to bloom in mid-March. Temperatures rose to the upper 60s and low 70s as the Flyers regrouped for the rest of the season.

The atmosphere was not like spring, however, in the Flyers' front office. Scarcely had the Flyers resumed playing when their coach, Wayne Cash-

John LeClair is stopped by Anaheim Mighty Ducks goalie Mikhail Shtalenkov in March 1998. In spite of some initial success under new coach Roger Neilson, the Flyers soon began to struggle.

man, was fired and replaced by Roger Neilson. Such changes are rare during the season, but the Flyers' management, still chafing from the 1997 Stanley Cup loss, wanted to give the team an edge as it headed toward postseason play.

Neilson arrived on March 9, and the Flyers immediately racked up a 3–0–2 record.

One encouraging fact was that LeClair had not missed a single game during the season. So far he had avoided the serious injuries that had hampered him earlier in his career. He had some close calls, though. In an early March game against the New York Islanders, one of the Islanders went after LeClair's knees in an effort to take him out of the game. Fortunately, the attempt produced only a penalty for roughing.

As a team, however, the Flyers began to play as if they were slightly damaged. During the rest of March they would have streaks of 3 and 4 wins in a row, but then they would be beaten by a team like Pittsburgh, which ended a 13-game losing streak with a 4–3 triumph over the Flyers. The sudden coaching change no longer seemed to be inspiring the Philadelphians.

In the loss to Pittsburgh, John LeClair scored his 42nd goal in the first period. Even as the team struggled, he was inching closer and closer to another 50-goal season.

In a game against the New Jersey Devils a few days later, LeClair lost what would have been his 43rd goal when the score was disallowed because part of his skate was in the crease.

The Flyers finished March with a 4–2 loss to the Carolina Hurricanes, the team's third loss in a row. "We didn't come to play as hard as we should have," LeClair said after the game. Referring to the heavy March schedule, he admitted that "fatigue is part of the problem, but it's not an excuse."

"We should be concerned," he added. "Some teams behind us could catch us."

At this point, with 11 games left to play in the regular season, hockey experts gave at least four other clubs—Detroit, New Jersey, Colorado, and Dallas—a better chance in the Stanley Cup playoffs than the Flyers. And it seemed that the Flyers might be pitted against the Buffalo Sabres in the first round of the playoffs. The Sabres' goalie was—who else?—the Dominator, Dominik Hasek.

The next day, however, the Flyers came back to life, and John LeClair tallied his 44th goal. He picked up a backhand pass from Rod Brind'Amour and whacked it into the net.

LeClair did it again the next night. He went to the net to rack up his 45th goal against the Chicago Blackhawks as the Flyers won, 3–2. LeClair, who had been in somewhat of a scoring slump since before the Olympics, was now clearly breaking out of it.

New Flyers player Mike Sillinger, who had joined the team just before the Olympics, had nothing but praise for the Gentle Giant. "I've learned to have a lot more appreciation for Johnny," said Sillinger. "You just don't realize how big and strong he is and how much he controls the puck out there."

LeClair now admitted that the Olympic Games and the hectic March schedule had taken their toll on him: "About a week or so ago, I started to feel better on the ice. Before that I wasn't really getting any chances. That's when things weren't going well at all. . . . I don't want to use any excuses. I just wasn't playing well."

In a game on April 8 against the Tampa Bay Lightning, LeClair scored his 47th and 48th goals, leaving him six games in the regular season to reach the 50-goal mark. His 48th was a perfect example of the importance of playing close to the net. The puck hit John's skate and bounced through goalie Mark Fitzpatrick's legs.

"That was just us getting rewarded," said LeClair after the game, in which the Flyers outshot the Lightning, 37–16. "I think we worked pretty hard.

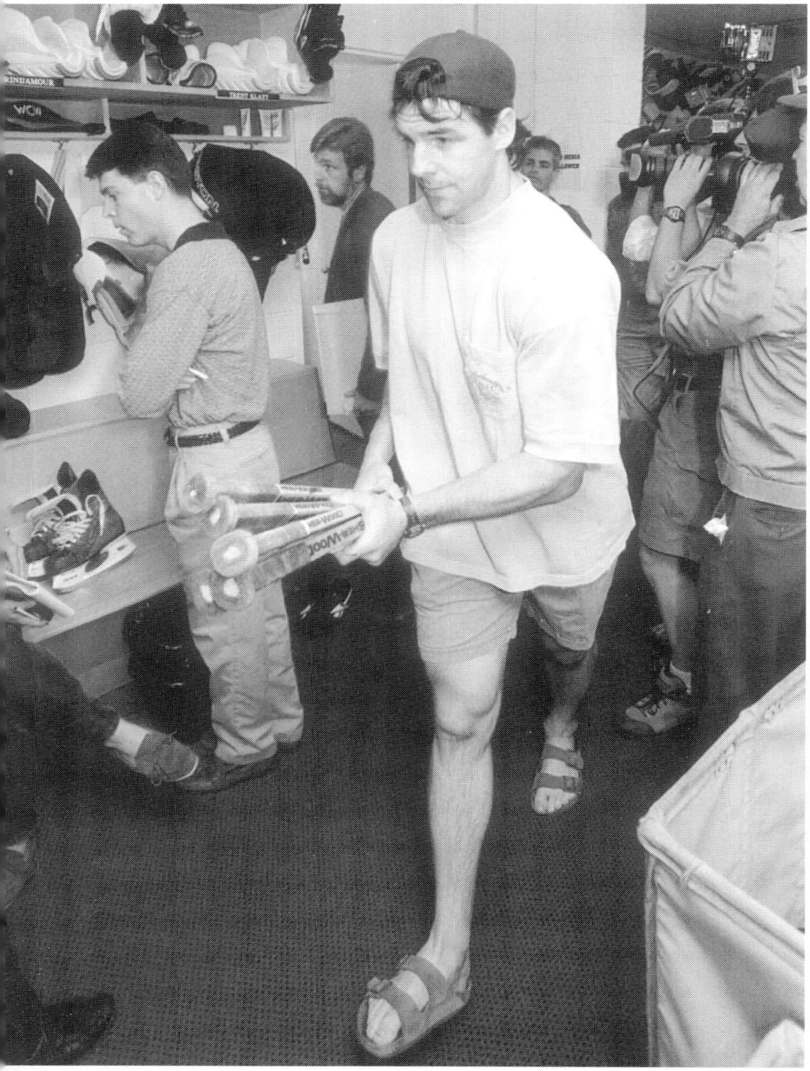

After the Flyers' elimination from the 1998 playoffs, John LeClair shows his dejection as he packs his sticks at the team's training complex.

We played a solid game tonight. He [Fitzpatrick] made some tremendous saves tonight, but nobody quit. We just kept coming back at them."

Three days later, the Flyers beat the Washington Capitals, and LeClair scored his 49th goal—a hard shot from the left circle into the short side of the goalie's net.

On April 13 John LeClair went into the record books when he scored a power-play goal against the Buffalo Sabres. The goalie, fittingly, was none other than Dominik Hasek. For the third season in a row, the man from little St. Albans, Vermont, had scored 50 goals during the regular season—the first American-born player to do so.

The 1997–98 season would end in disappointment for the Philadelphia Flyers. Led by Olympic hero Hasek, the Sabres eliminated the Flyers in the first round of the playoffs. Still, it was a memorable season for John LeClair.

Whatever his setbacks, LeClair had continued to demand the most from himself. Losing, of course, is part of any game; but as Coach Cashman had said, the best teams and the best players do not find it acceptable. John LeClair's winning attitude will continue to carry him successfully through the rest of his NHL career.

Whether his team wins or loses, whether he makes millions of dollars or not, to everyone who knows him John LeClair is a winner.

RANGERS
35
10
SHER

Regular Guy and Role Model

Hockey, like other professional sports, is a game of role models. School-age kids look up to the best players and try to imitate them. It is not surprising, then, that youth hockey participation has been rising throughout the state of Vermont. This development is attributed to the success of John LeClair, Vermont's native son.

Mark McGinn, president of the Vermont State Amateur Hockey Association, said that membership in the association has doubled in five years to over 5,000 children. "John is a major factor" in that increase, McGinn believes.

Role models are important even for young professionals. When Colin Forbes joined the Flyers as a rookie, he gladly admitted that he used LeClair as a role model. Even though Forbes is only six years younger than LeClair, he watched LeClair's every move, learning how to become a true NHL player.

John LeClair's hustle and determination have made him a role model for younger players.

"I try to do things like him as far as things on and off the ice," Forbes said. "Obviously, I'm never going to be able to shoot the puck like him. But I can go to the net and use my size to establish position. Right now, he is one of the top three players in the league. He's the type of player you want to follow."

With his skill, his hard work, and most of all his dedication to playing the game well and winning, John LeClair is a fitting example for any young hockey player. Many athletes would consider that good enough. Many professionals even insist that they should not be expected to act as role models for anyone. LeClair, though, takes his responsibilities seriously, and he doesn't believe that they end when he steps off the ice.

After a grueling NHL season, LeClair returns to his hometown for a summer break. With his wife, Christina; his daughter, MacKenzie; his son, Calvin; and their two Labradors, Abbie and Archie, he enjoys getting back to the traditional life of tiny St. Albans, where the multimillionaire hockey player can be just a regular guy among his old friends and neighbors.

Even so, summer is never a time for doing nothing if you are John LeClair. When he's not playing hockey, he works with the John LeClair Foundation, which he established in 1993 to aid the needy children of Vermont. The foundation raises funds and gives approximately half of what it collects each year to youth organizations. The other half is put in a trust, where it earns more money that the foundation can use to spend on more children.

With John as host, the foundation sponsors an annual Charity Celebrity Golf Tournament, combined with a Celebrity Dinner and Auction. Over the years the celebrities have included a number of John's Flyers teammates, as well as hockey greats Patrick Roy, Martin Brodeur, and Bobby Orr. In 1997 alone, the two events raised nearly $150,000 for needy children.

The foundation has helped as many as 26 organizations in a year, and its projects are varied. It has helped pregnant women receive good health care and education. It has aided terminally ill children. It has funded a resource directory for preventing child abuse and a video for a program aimed at expectant parents and at-risk families. It has contributed to educational programs dealing with drug and alcohol abuse. Its donations have helped improve the pediatric units at health care centers. It has assisted a Teen Futures Project at a youth center. When one youth association lost its sports equipment in a fire, the foundation contributed money to buy new equipment.

Whatever his other commitments, LeClair has always found time to respond to his fans.

In February 1997 the Philadelphia Sports Writers Association recognized these achievements. The sports writers gave John LeClair their Humanitarian of the Year Award for his work with his foundation. Typically, in a statement that he issued afterward, he was modest about this honor: "To be recognized as the leading humanitarian sports

John LeClair visits the King Street Youth Center in Burlington, Vermont, one of the institutions that he has aided through the John LeClair Foundation.

person among all athletes from the Philadelphia area is a distinction I gladly accepted. However, it was immediately clear the award did not belong to me. It belonged to the Foundation."

Clearly, John LeClair is a player who has not let his success go to his head.

STATISTICS

		Regular Season					Playoffs				
Season	Team	GP	G	A	PTS	PIM	GP	G	A	PTS	PIM
1990–91	Mon	10	2	5	7	2	3	0	0	0	0
1991–92	Mon	59	8	11	19	14	8	1	1	2	4
1992–93	Mon	72	19	25	44	33	20	4	6	10	14
1993–94	Mon	74	19	24	43	32	7	2	1	3	8
1994–95	Mon/Phi	46	26	28	54	30	15	5	7	12	4
1995–96	Phi	82	51	46	97	64	11	6	5	11	6
1996–97	Phi	82	50	47	97	58	19	9	12	21	10
1997–98	Phi	82	51	36	87	32	5	1	1	2	8
Totals		507	226	222	448	265	88	28	33	61	54

GP games played
G goals scored
A assists
PTS points (goals plus assists)
PIM penalties in minutes

CHRONOLOGY

1969	John LeClair born on July 5 in St. Albans, Vermont.
1975	Starts skating at age six.
1984–87	Plays high school hockey at Bellows Free Academy in St. Albans; in his final two seasons, scores 85 goals in 45 games.
1987	Drafted by the Montreal Canadiens of the NHL, but elects to attend college.
1987–91	Stars on the hockey team at the University of Vermont; named an Eastern Collegiate Athletic Association second-team All-Star in 1990–91.
1991	Debuts with the Montreal Canadiens.
1993	Wins the Stanley Cup with the Montreal Canadiens.
1994–95	Traded to the Philadelphia Flyers; named First-Team NHL All-Star.
1995–96	Scores 51 goals in the season; named Second-Team NHL All-Star.
1996	Helps the U.S. team win the World Cup.
1996–97	Scores 50 goals in the season; named Second-Team NHL All-Star.
1997	Helps lead the Philadelphia Flyers to the Stanley Cup finals.
1998	Plays on Team USA during 1998 winter Olympics in Nagano, Japan; at the end of the NHL season, becomes the first American-born player to score 50 or more goals for three seasons in a row.

FURTHER READING

Davidson, John. *Hockey for Dummies.* Foster City, Calif.: IDG Books Worldwide, 1997.

Hollander, Zander. *The Complete Encyclopedia of Hockey.* Detroit: Gale Research, 1993.

Liebman, Glenn. *Hockey Shorts.* Chicago: Contemporary Books, 1996.

The National Hockey League. *Hockey Rules in Pictures.* New York: Perigee, 1992.

Rosenbaum, Dave, editor. *Hockey Stars Presents The Hockey Book.* Ambler, Pa.: London, 1997.

Rossiter, Sean. *Hockey the NHL Way: Goal Scoring.* Vancouver: Greystone, 1997.

About the Author

Phelan Powell has worked as a daily correspondent for the *Michigan City News-Dispatch.* Earlier, Phelan wrote feature articles and created a cartoon strip for college newspapers. Currently Phelan is working on other books for Chelsea House Publishers.

PICTURE CREDITS: © 1998 Allsport USA/Craig Melvin/All Rights Reserved: p. 9; AP/Wide World Photos: pp. 6, 11, 20, 24, 26, 28, 30, 34, 36, 40, 43, 46, 49, 52, 54, 57; Courtesy, Bill DiLillo, University of Vermont: pp. 12–13, 18; Courtesy, John LeClair Foundation; photograph by Wayne Tarr: p. 58; Courtesy, Robert LeClair: p. 15; Courtesy, Philadelphia Flyers: p. 2; Reuters/Corbis-Bettmann: p. 23.

INDEX